Beneath the Dragonwood Trees

In the Beginning

An Original Musical Fairytale Cantata

Book, Lyrics, Music, Illustrations
By Margot Elaine Jones

LOrD & DOONEY PrESS

San Rafael, California
www.margotelainejones.com

Publisher's Note:

This is a work of fiction. Names, characters, places, and incidents are a product of the author's imagination. Locales and public names are sometimes used for atmospheric purposes. Any resemblance to actual people, living or dead, or to businesses, companies, events, institutions, or locales is completely coincidental.

Ordering Information:

Quantity sales. Special discounts are available on quantity purchases by corporations, associations, and others. For details, contact the "Special Sales Department" at the address above.

Beneath the Dragonwood Trees / Margot Elaine Jones. —1st ed.
ISBN 978-1-7328166-1-9 paperback
ISBN 978-1-7328166-2-6 ebook

Dedicated to the Master Magician
of all things
great and small

"He, who is above the wise and the wicked."

—Whisper

TABLE OF CONTENTS

To enjoy the songs and music, please download a free QR scanner on your phone and then use it to scan the many QR codes in the book.

Cast of Characters

Allesendra . . . . . . The Storyteller
Beanie Fox . . . . Allesendra's Pal
Farfull Bear . . . . Allesendra's Pal
Fairyfoot . . . . Queen Of Fairies
Peter . . . . Nine-Year-Old Boy
Lavinia . . . . Peter's Grandmother
Vernon . . . . Peter's Grandfather
Sire Bumbles . . . . The Badger Man
Purrina Kitten-Cat . . . . Peter's Best Pal
Pancho Duck . . . . Peter's Pal
Lillabell Bird . . . . Peter's Pal
Ravenous E. Lee . . . . The Big Bad Wolf
Wickety . . . . The Witch
Dusty . . . . The Witch's Broom
Murrell . . . . A Hunter
Bucky . . . . A Hunter
Otus . . . . A Hunter
JB . . . . A Hunter
Paddy McDougal . . . . King Of Leprechauns
Finnegan . . . . Leprechaun
Bonnie Jean . . . . Leprechaun
Whisper . . . . The Wood Nymph
Whisper The Great . . . . The Impostor
Beatralean . . . . . Fairyfoot's Trusted Agent
Brendlewood . . Fairyfoot's Trusted Agent
Tanter, the Unicorn . . Fairyfoot's Steed

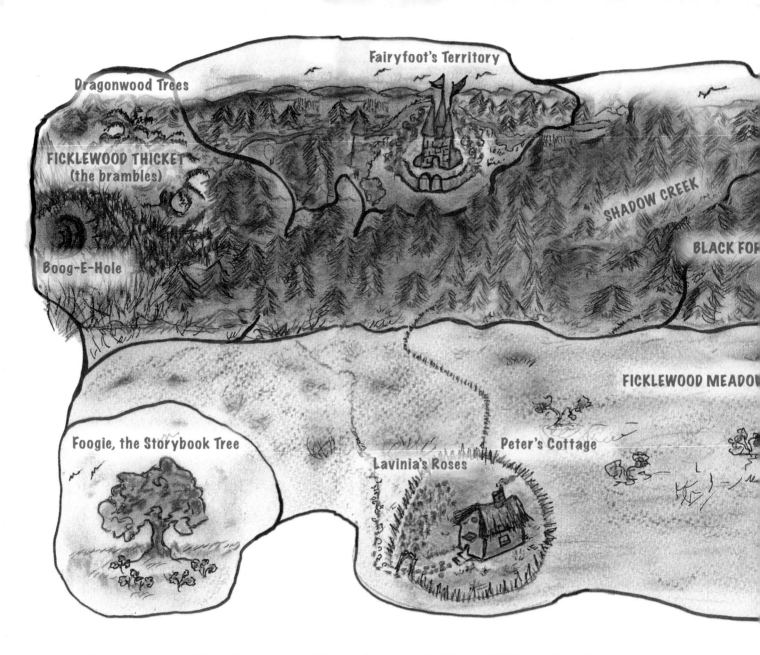

Once upon a time long ago, there lived a BOY, a BIRD, a DUCK, and a CAT. Just a stone's throw from the Black Forest of Ficklewood. Three shakes of a lamb's tail past Witch Wickety's hut. Beyond the Down-Under, where the sun don't shine, the trees don't grow, where there are no stars, and

the wind don't blow. A journey past the Boog-E-Hole, where giants lie in wait and naughty children quake at the very mention of the place. Into the meadow, Ficklewood Meadow, where lives the Boy, his pals...and a tale you will not forget.

My name is Allesendra, and I am a storyteller.

Every afternoon, just as the sun peeks over my sycamore tree, Foogie, I climb to my favorite spot. Way up high, in a big, broad, leafy branch that looks like a nest and read to my favorite companions: Farfull Bear and Beanie Fox. Oh! And of course, my little feathered friends…the Birds.

Now then, close your eyes and imagine a flock of sparrows and finches, circling a massive sycamore tree…my sycamore tree—Foogie.

"That is right, I am yours!"

"Come on Farfull, one more branch."

"Are we too late?"

You're right on time. Now settle down both of you. Farfull, you sit right next to me and Beanie, you can sit right here on my lap with Book. There are fairies at the bottom of my garden. They have entrusted me with a magical book and while I read, the pages turn themselves. I'll read this one, *Beneath the Dragonwood Trees.*

Chapter One
The Beginning

Beyond the Thicket and through the Dragonwood Trees...lives a witch by the name of Wickety, a strict, sullen, stick of a woman with hair red as fire and a temper to match. Especially when she was kept awake all night by pesky, pecking sparrows on her thatched roof. She rose from her bed of straw, scrambled out of her hut and stumbled over to her magic broom, Dusty.

"OY! WAKE-UP BUPKES!"

He was on the porch, propped up against the door, snoring. She grabbed the groggy broom and gave it a swift kick in the bristles.

"OY! Wake-Up BUPKES! An' watch where you're flyin-k!
Or you'll eat DUST-fa-dinner!"

The Broom pooped out smoke with a jerk and sputter as if it had a motor. She hopped on it and flew up to her rooftop shaking her fist at the noisy sparrows.

"Ooooy! Ah-russs-ka-Schmuckin-dorfel! Off my rooftop! Mit d' pecking-n' scratchink or I'll bake you into a pie mit four-and-twenty-BLACK BIRDS! OFF my ROOFTOP! OFF my ROOFTOP!!"

Dusty almost hit the chimney.

"OOOY! "OOOY! "OOOY! You're flying like ah bat from Beelzebub!"

He paid no attention to her and flipped her upside down. Round and around the hut he flew. Faster and faster.

"This is so much fun!"

He slammed past a prickly tree just outside Wickety's bedroom window. She was hanging by her toes trying to stop him! She hooped and hollered!

"OOOY! "OOOY! Ooooy! Ah-russs-ka-Schmuckin-dorfell!! You'll pay fa-this!"

He careened into a flock of birds.

"WOOOO-HAAA! HOP-DE-DOODLE!"

"DOWN! MIT-YOU! DOWN!"

The Sparrows chattered among themselves, watching the out-of-control mishaps.

"We better get out of here. Peep, Peep!
She's gonna' bake us into one of those pies."

Off they flew. Wickety and Dusty landed with a bump and a thud on the front porch.

"YAH! MISHEGAS!"

She was very angry.

"Ah-russs-ka-Schmuckin-dorfell!!"

"HOP-DE-DOODLE! Sorry!"

Dusty stood erect, in front of the door, twitching his bristles as she continued to scold him.

"YA-know from nothink-from-FLYINK! Into the hut mit-you!
Clear away the schmitzig! VASH DISHES! There's no breakfast
'til yah-FINISH-Schmuckin-dorfell."

She brushed a large spider from her door as he slumped into the kitchen to do her bidding. BUT! When she wasn't looking he had a big ol' smile on his bristles, because. . . after all, it was so much fun.

He was surprised to find the dishes flying all about the kitchen. They landed in a neat pile in the sink. Two chairs shoved themselves into place under the little wooden table and the pump handle at the sink began gushing water for the dishes.

Wickety trounced about giving the old broom orders.

"FASTER! FASTER! FASTER!"

He dutifully swept the floor and brushed away the cobwebs. Suddenly there came a loud knock at the door.

"A klog iz mir! WHO'S-ZAT KNOCKINK-AT MY DOOR? MORFUS...The BLUE
GIANT? OY! Shouldn' happin' but some-times happin'. SPEAK UP!"

"I'm ah lost boy!"

"PETER PAN?"

"No! Yah see...he's about flying! I gotta' catch a Wolf!"

Wickety threw open the door to see a wiry, tussle-haired boy in grey overalls, brown lace-up boots, and a checkered scarf around his neck. Cowering behind him was a bird, a cat, and a duck. The cat whispered in the boy's ear:

"Remember what that Mr. Bumbles said."

"I'll be careful."

He took a deep breath and bravely stepped forward as Wickety leapt out of the hut. She grabbed hold of the scarf around his neck before he could speak.

"Com-ee-yah! What'-z-ah'-matter! Cat got-cha tongue?"

"Ah, I...ah...NO! Peter! My name is...Peter."

"WHAT-EVER! Um not interested. Second thought, watz-yah business HERE?"

"We're lost."

"Lost are yah?"

Wickety was so tall, she had to bend down to get a closer look at him. The feisty cat peeked out from behind him.

"Mee-oow excuse me, but I can explain everything, don't-cha-know."

"An' who are you? NEVER MIND! I'm not interested."

She poked them with her gnarly fingers.

"Ah BOY! Ah DUCK! Ah CAT!"

"Meeee-OOW! Excuse me, if-ya-don't mind, but, my name is Purrina an' I'm ah Kitten-cat! Ah kitten...CAT."

"What'z-difference! You're ah CAT, that's not ah kitten, but ya-ah kitten-cat, NONSENSE! Makes NO sense ta-me!"

"Well! Actually!"

"Not interested. On second thought, I might be interested, if you were, saaay, related to Puss n' Boots?"

"OH! Third cousin once removed on my mother's side, on my father's side, well, that doesn't count, actually. Uncle Bootzy's my favorite cousin don't cha-know, that's his nickname, Bootzy. That's-on a-count-ah-the-fact-he always wears BOOTS!"

"Never MIND! Um-not interested."

Wickety shoved Peter aside and tried to be polite, poking them once again with her boney fingers.

"Ah, this one's ah CAT-kitten, kitten-CAT, what-ever! Duck and ah Boy. Humm...I don't recognize your story. Um afraid yah NOT in my fairytale, who's-who anthology book. Ya-have-ta understand it's my duty, now that Mother Goose is gone, ta- write ya-story."

"Well, yah see we're lost an' Grandfather will be looking for me, us."

Wickety stomped her foot three times, to quicken her memory and twitched her nose.

"Hummm—farafinkel, now I remember! I think I know who yah talkin' about. Yah stories about a VOLF who's name begins with…RRRRR! RAVENOUS! He goes by the name of Ravenous, ta be exact. Sorry ta-tell-yah…can't put-cha-story-in-the book, till yah finish yah episode, but! There's someone might help."

Peter bravely stepped closer to her.

"Who?"

"Sire Bumbles."

"Oh, Ma-heaven-sakes, we've already seen him, haven't we, Purrina?"

Wickety peeked around Purrina to see a beautiful bird with feathers as lovely as a rainbow.

"An Whatz-ya-name?"

"Her name's Lillabell, in-case you're in-ter-ested. She's from the South and queen of all the birds. Isn't that right, Lillabell? We're not related but, we're best-est friends, very hungry I might add."

Purrina shoved Lillabell in front of Wickety.

"Wal-say-somethin,' Lillabell."

"Well ah-would if ah-could…that is, if you've a mind ta' let me…"

"Meeee-OOW! We're wondering if you have anything to EAT!" Cause we've been climbing and swatting through this forest for the longest time over 'n over 'n-nover, nove, over, 'n-over, over, nover, NOVER…nove…"

"OY!!"

Wickety's hair spiked.

"I need ah drink, ah Spiveys Pepson with a dash ah coyote pepper! Yah-given' me horse pimples!"

Purrina backed away with a pout on her whiskers. Wickety spun around and grabbed a hold of Peter.

"Listen-ta-me! An' put this in yah-can-noodle!"

Wickety opened her mouth to sing and the trees trembled.

WICKETY'S SONG

Com-ee-yah!

Beware of the VOLF I'm-tell-ink-U.
I've seen his hairy claws.
Beware of the VOLF I'm tell-ink-U...
Those great big teeth and jaw...

He licks, he lacks, he clicks, he clacks,
He's almost ten feet tall...
Beware of the VOLF I'm tellink you...
He'll EAT you! Bones an' all...

The bird and the duck hid behind a tree as she continued her ominous song.

I used to go on tippy-toes for fear he might be
Lurking near, Oy! Those ears.
I closed the cupboards and bolted the doors
And locked the chimney too

Even the chimney flue
What's a girl ta' do
I crawled into bed without ginger bread
And I was hungry too
But I was scared, black n' blue,
Of those beady little eyes and that slimy, little, smile,"

She lunged behind the tree to fetch Lillabell and the duck.

"Com'ee-yah!"

Beware of the VOLF he's got bad breath,
It'll take yah down to ya-shoes,
Beware of the volf I'm tell-ink-U,
You won't be going ta-school,

He licks, he lacks, he clicks, he clacks,
He's almost ten feet tall...
Beware of the wolf I'm tell-ink-U.
He'll eat you!

BONES...

"That Wolf has got-ta get out-ta the forest I'm tellink' yah, he's a schmuck. Here, there, everywhere. He's gonna bring the Hunters! You got-ta get out-ta here!

"AN' ALLLLLLL... Com'ee-yah!"

She gathered them all around.

"Vell? The WOLF'S ah shmendrik! Shouldn-'appin'-but zometimez-appinz."

Purrina twitched her ears.

"He's ah... smuc-smick-what?"

"Never mind."

Peter took hold of Purrina's little paw.

"Ah! Gee-whiz! I'm not afraid of ah silly ol' WOLF! Anyways, I got-ta find him! The Wolf that is, but we got lost."

"Yeah!"

"We need help don't-chu-know, before it's too late an' his grandpa has ta' find us an' we're in a peck ah trouble an' Peter can't talk to us an' we can't talk ta' him, an' no one can talk to anyone...an..."

"OY! VEY! OY"

Frantically spinning around, Wickety yelled!

"Hip-Skies-Hanky-Panky PEPSON! I'll take the WHOOOOLE bottle!"

She yanked a small bottle from her pocket and gulped it down while kicking up her heels.

"Now, Sire Bumbles is the one ta' help-yah! But! There's ah storm comin'. Not to mention the VOLF! Good luck! You'll need it!"

She pulled open the door to the hut and slammed it behind her.

"Quack! Ay carumba! That Wickety! D'-dispositions, 'es very bad. Ang-I don' gonna-like-dis!! Quack-quack!"

"Well, she is a good Witch, even if she doesn't act like one."

"Papacita was right! Volviendo loco! Volviendo LOCO! I feel it in my bone-z ang d' bone-z never wrong!"

"Don't worry Pancho, I got my compus."

Reaching into his pocket, he pulled out a silver instrument the size of a pocket watch. It had two eyes and a mouth, and its golden hand spun around. Then it chuckled and blinked at Peter.

"At your service, master. Wherever you wish to go."

"Well...your gauge is pointing due North, so...we'll go North! That's where the Wolf is, I'll bet! Everybody get closer an' listen. If any one of us gets lost or separated, we'll give the secret signal, you know, pow-wow-ug-ah-waga-omm-pow-wow. Got it?"

"We got it!"

"Ay! Ay! Ay!"

Pancho snatched his sombrero off and tossed it to the ground.

"Dis-is no-gonna-be-easy! I got d'z feelings in d' bonzes ang d' feelings in d' bonzes..."

Everyone repeated the same thing.

"Is never WRONG!"

"Si amigos."

"AH! Come ON! Pancho! I'll catch that Wolf, get my Badge of Honor an' we'll have ah GOOD time! You'll see."

"Na' jus-don't you worry Pancho, darlin'. We'll be home before the rooster crows!"

"Lillabell! It's 2pm don't-cha-know."

"Oh! My! Silly me. He already has...hasn't he? Crowed, ah mean!"

Lillabell picked up the sombrero and sweetly placed it back on his head.

"AH come ON! Times a wastin'!"

They performed their "regimented, fancy hand slap," linked arms and headed for the forest with renewed vigor, singing and dancing.

SHADOW CREEK SONG

Near Shadow Creek and Billberry Brook,
it's not so far away...

Lickity split an' licorice sticks
There's plenty of time for play...

Over the meadow and into the woods,
we haven't got time to tarry,

Billberry Brook and Shadow Creek,
Billberry Brook and Shadow Creek,

Shadow Creek...

Just look at them...off they go, deeper and deeper into the forest. Now I need to stop and explain a few things.

"Ah! Just keep readin', won't that explain what comes next?"

Well...according to the fairies in my garden there's a bit of the story missing. You see, Peter was told not to go into the forest, but he just couldn't help himself. The trees were so beautiful and the sky so blue and golly-gee-wiz maybe...just maybe he could catch the wolf. After all, that particular wolf has been a menace to everyone in Fairyland and thereabouts. And why shouldn't he catch the wolf? Well if he could catch that wolf instead of the Hunters, he could win a Badge of Honor, something he's always wanted. That's why he disobeyed his grandparents. But, once in the forest, he should have listened to Pancho.

Soon after leaving Wickety's hut the sun faded, and dark clouds began to form. They all tried to find shelter, but they ended up in a very dense part of the woods. Thunderclouds rolled across the sky. And what's worse, they accidently crawled into Ficklewood Thicket, a towering, quagmire of brambles and trees with UGLY FACES. A marsh, a swamp, a bog—a dark, dank, soggy, miserable place to end up. Once you've entered the Thicket... you must beware. The Boogieman fell into that monstrous hole because of his bad deeds. And that monstrous hole is in that THICKET...where the sun don't shine an' the wind don't blow.

"Oh! My! Heavens, Al-wa-sendra! That's why the fairies call wit-da-BOOG-E-HOLE! Well I...I guess I yike-to hear da-west-of-da story."

"Well...it was so dark they were all confused. Pancho had to let go of Lillabell when a thorny branch caught hold of his tail. Peter was trying to free his shirt from a carnivorous weed when he lost Purrina. The secret signal echoed back and forth through the Thicket.

"Pow-wow-ug-ah-waga-omm-pow-wow."

First Pancho, then Lillabell, and Purrina. Even though Peter returned the signal, they couldn't find each other. Some of the animals and fairies could hear Peter's secret signals echoing through the forest, but none of them were brave enough to venture into the towering brambles.

"Pow-wow-ug-ah-waga-omm-pow-wow."

"Pow-wow-ug-ah-waga-omm-pow-wow."

That evening, Peter's grandfather headed for the forest and sent for the Hunters. The bumbling Hunters tramped through the forest like a plague of locusts—overloaded with muskets, knapsacks dry goods, hunting gear, and unnecessary trinkets. A musket fired accidently, and they collided into each other. Scrambling about senselessly, they gathered their wits about them and tippy-toed down the path, muskets drawn, until they thought they saw the wolf! They fell over each other trying to escape and headed for safety in the meadow where they soon fell asleep under the trees.

Peter's grandfather played his flute in hopes that Peter would hear it. Unfortunately...tired to the bone, he had to return home without him.

The hours tick-tocked the moon across the sky for midnight to come. Lillabell's beautiful wings were trapped in the brambles and thorns. She could hear the echo of signals off in the distance, but why couldn't Pancho find her?

Why couldn't any of them find her? Unable to free her wings, she pecked the stickers out of her feathers.

"Oh! Dear Master Magician of all things great and small, whatever shall ah do?"

After a while, a peaceful feeling came over her and she fell asleep.

In the late hour, Peter had to wrestle his shirttail away from a mean, nasty bramble with an ugly face. He crawled through the muddy Thicket all night, covered with scratches from thorns and brambles, but he kept returning to the same spot he had previously marked with his scarf. He forced his muddy hands into his pocket for Compus. It was cranky, full of mud, and its eyes were shut.

"WAKE-UP! wake up, Compus!"

"I cannot, Master, my instruments are too damp.
Day is...night-time cometh, north is south, east try west,
west is best... OH! I don't know."

Peter tapped on its face, but it gave a sigh and fell back to sleep. All Peter could do was wait for the storm to end.

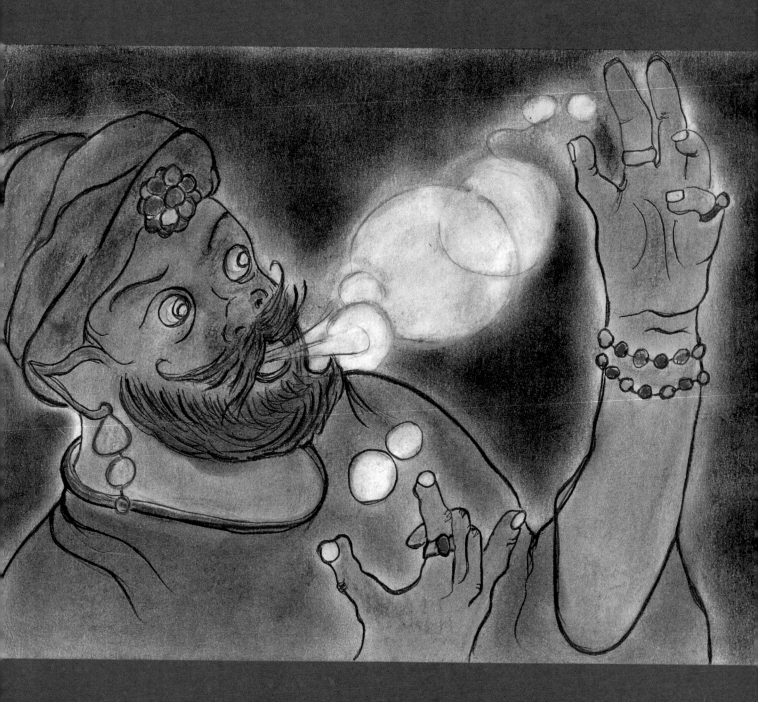

Chapter Two
Whisper the Great

The kingdom of Fairyfoot lies within the boundaries of Ficklewood Forest, five miles to the East and five miles to the West of Shadow Creek. The castle is magnificent and dutifully protected by a wall of magical wisteria called the Chingly-Changly. It blooms a purple flower and its thick, intertwining limbs can hold captive any unwanted guest.

Fairyfoot is Queen of Fairies. She is known for her beauty and wisdom. All in Fairyland look to her for guidance.

The hour is late. She is seated at her desk amidst an array of glorious flowers, quill pen in hand.

Out of the blue, a stout Leprechaun by the name of Paddy McDougal bolts into the room. He's a bit confused and out of breath.

"Majesty! I've news from King Boom. The Boy is gone, missing in the Thicket...Down Under. Most likely on another search for the Wolf."

"Not again! Quickly! Fetch Bumbles! And I'll summon Whisper. The storm is settling. I'll leave immediately. Off with you!"

He turned on his heels sixteen times and disappeared.

Fairyfoot removed three small golden bags from one of the drawers and placed them neatly in her bodice. She moved toward a large window in the room and opened both shutters. The night sky is filled with dark clouds. Spreading her glorious wings, she drifts out of the window, high above the trees.

Fairyfoot flew to King Boom Oak's territory, the tallest and wisest tree in the forest. His spying branches can see far and wide, ten miles to the East and ten miles to the West. He is a safe meeting place for the fairies and elves of Ficklewood Forest. Unwanted creatures find it very difficult to climb King Boom, including the wolf. Fairyfoot lightly descended onto one of Boom's massive branches and gently stroked his bark with her lovely hand. Boom awakened, rolling his large wooden eyes.

"Good eve to you, King Boom Oak."

"And to you fair maiden, Queen of Fairies."

"I've come to meet Whisper, for I have summoned him. The Boy is lost again and Whisper's incantations and obedience to the laws of the One will be of great service."

"I know him not."

"They say he's black as night, with hair as white as snow to his knees. Others say he is of elfin kind, not a wood nymph at all. But I must beware, for there are many who claim to be this Whisper."

"Have no Fear! My branches shall protect you. They are strong enough to shake down the wind."

Suddenly, a huge puff of smoke curled around her. Boom Oak's leaves trembled as if by magic, and a wood nymph appeared seated on the branch right next to her. It was so unexpected.

"SALAAM! SALOOM! SILLABEM! I am Whisper the GREAT! Possessed of a mighty power! I've come to assist you for I hear-tell you are in need of my person! Tis true! My magic is far reaching, even beyond the realms of Fairyland."

Fairyfoot took note of his outlandish headdress, his golden rings and earrings of the rarest kind on almost every finger. She raised her hand for his attention and spoke in a soft manner.

"If you please, I am in need of one who can fulfill my..."

"Say no more! Say no more! Look you here! I shall cause that fir tree to up-root and run away."

"Please...I have a plan for Peter and his companions. You must understand, the Wolf..."

"WHAT! You seem blasé! Apathetic! Unimpressed! I challenge you to look above the trees! My dragon comes forth. I have commanded it to do your bidding!"

"But I have no need for dragons." The dragon hovered above Fairyfoot.

"Shall I strike her, master?"

"Be gone! Be GONE I say!" The dragon disappeared.

Whisper thought it great sport and chuckled. With a wave of his hand, the dragon re-appeared.

"Maybe this will find you more enthusiastic! Grab her, Dragon! Carry her high above the forest into the bowels of the North Wind."

Boom Oak shook his branches to the very core of his roots in hopes of stopping the dragon, but he was rendered powerless. The dragon took Fairyfoot up in its great claws-higher than she had ever flown before. Over the valleys and hills, high into the clouds.

The North Wind whistled as they drew near to its mighty force. All manner of things were caught up in its dark hurricane: trees and carts, toys and boxes, rooftops and carriages, papers and houses, old tin cans and rivers of sand, boulders and bushels, ribbons and feathers, bottles and pans.

The dragon delivered Fairyfoot into the bowels of the Wind as he was commanded.

She swirled and tumbled and twisted and turned. The North Wind felt sorry for her and tried to soften its blows as it sang its mournful song. After quite a time, she was returned to one of Boom's large branches. Whisper found his magic very entertaining and he laughed so hard, Boom tried to swat him off his branch, but he could not. Fairyfoot was composed and lovely, not a hair out of place after such an ordeal.

> "Your magic is self-serving, it has no purpose. I rather doubt you are Whisper."

"Trees bend to my will. I can silence the wind and raise the waters of the sea."

"To glorify your ego. Not for the betterment of anything or anyone, I'm afraid."

The song of a nightingale, clear and sweet played upon the evening breeze and another wood nymph magically appeared. Fairyfoot took note of his bright eyes and dark skin, his goatskin jacket and green polished boots— a soft-spoken, gentle soul.

"Good eve to you fair maiden, Queen of Fairies. You have summoned me."

Whisper the Great scoffed.

"HA! POPPY-COCK! I am Whisper The Great! Your magic is no match for mine! My Whisper can be heard around the world!

"That is...when I whisper."

The Wood Nymph paid him no mind and extended his hand politely to Fairyfoot. A smile crossed her lips.

"Art thou...truly Whisper?"

"Indeed I am. Good eve to you."

"And so to you. As you can see, there are others who claim to be Whisper. Therefore, if you are willing, I wish to put you to the test."

Whisper the Great laughed wildly.

"You doubt my authenticity! I shall pass any test you have to offer.

Give ME the fairy dust! I shall spread it around the WORLD! Let me rule FAIRYLAND! And I'll make known its greatness throughout the Kingdoms of the Earth! I...am the Master Magician!"

Fairyfoot watched him twiddle his thumbs arrogantly. After a moment he became impatient with her, flailing his arms all about.

"Well! WELL! WHAT? WHAT say YOU?"

She turned away from him and gave her full attention to the other Whisper.

"Now then, If...thou art Whisper, meaning...you, sir, with the polished boots and fine coat, would you kindly answer these two questions?"

"Indeed, my Queen."

"First, who planted the moon in a black firmament and scattered countless diamonds. Then lit He a ball of fire and separated sky from seas?"

"Clearly the Master Magician of all things Great and Small. Of that which can be seen and that which cannot be seen. He, who is above the wise and the wicked."

Pleased with his answer, she spread her wings with delight.

"Tis' so. Truly you are Whisper." Her eyes sparkled.

"Many claim to be and present magic from a wand."

She turned to the imposter.

"As did you sir, but I say Nay. Your use of magic and free will is

blasphemous. Tis' true, I've the use of magical tools, but I know my place. You, sir, abuse it."

She spread her wings as she spoke, and her eyes sparkled.

"There is only one Master Magician. His breath brings forth the rising of the sun, and his song is in the life of all living things."

"Then all is DONE with you! I am off to places where I am well-received... and well-respected."

He disappeared in a puff of smoke, just as he had arrived.

Fairyfoot carefully pulled from her bodice of satin lace, three golden bags for Whisper.

"Here is fairy dust which I have prepared, filled with jasmine leaves, marigold, alkane, tannin root, shoots of jonquils, and redbud ground to perfection."

"Humm...ingredients to fast put sleep bedraggled beasts of prey and save young mortals gone astray."

"Tis' SO! Now I pray you, sprinkle its powder throughout the forest, so that, for a time the Wolf sleeps. Tis' true, its power is short-lived, but when the Wolf awakens, as he is about his mischief, he shall fall asleep, then awaken, then fall asleep, and awaken once again and so on. He sleeps! Awakes! Sleeps! Awakens! Tis' great folly!"

"Indeed!"

"Then...I shall see to it Sire Bumbles rescues Peter."

Fairyfoot spreads her wings with great relief.

"Kind sir, thou art swift as wind, far more so than I. Is it true, they say your incantations and your whisper...can be heard throughout the forest and beyond?"

"So I am told."

"Truly you are Whisper!"

"Clearly...as you are Queen of Fairies."

"Kind sir...this deed is done."

She drifted above him and bid him farewell.

Quickly he opened the golden bags of fairy dust and began casting the spell, journeying throughout the forest, his voice a deep whisper permeating the woods.

"Jasmine dust, marigold, alkane, tannin root, weave this numbing spell within...Hold the jaunty Wolf. Bind his claws."

The fairy dust glistened in the moonlight.

"Go now...shoots of jonquils and redbud, lightly in the mist."

Whisper blew the fairy dust high above the trees and with a deep whisper that permeated the forest and all about, said:

"BE GONE!"

Within the twinkle of an eye, like a phantom he disappeared.

"Oh! What about Peter? Will-abell, Pancho, and Poa-wena?"

Well...Beanie, time marched with a tick and a tock, pulling the moon across the sky and the sun rose on a new morning. Purrina awakened exhausted and fearful that she would never find her way out of the twisted brambles. She wiped the sleep from her eyes and began her search for Peter again. From time to time she stopped and licked her fur where stickers had bruised her, unaware that the wolf was in the Thicket, crouched in a patch of weeds, inches away. The scent of Purrina tickled past his nose and he rose up on the ready to catch her.

"OH! No! She bett-ur-run! Oh! But she can't!"

Well, there is one saving grace in all of this, Beanie. Ravenous Wolf is an awkward beast, and although his frightful looks would scare any unsuspecting traveler or fairy, he for the most part, is well...full of "blarney." He once bragged of eating four goblins and a goat at a single meal. He boasted he swallowed scores of birds and proudly proclaimed:

> "Ah washed them critters down with a shot of beetle juice. Ma-teeth can grind the bones of any animal, large or small, into a fine, fine powder, for which ah then use as a seasoning for ma-culinary delights."

Farfull's ears perked up.

"Does he GRIND their BONES?"

Well...so he says. But most elves and goblins in Fairyland, and those humans living just outside its entrance, complain that he's nothing but trouble—a menace—and that those Hunters are dim-witted bubble-heads when it comes to the business of catching him.

"Oh! Durr-all-waf-frad of-um. But what about Purrina?"

The wolf continued to slither through the muck and mire, stalking her. As Purrina crawled closer, the wolf licked his chops. She licked her paws. His red eyes glistened. Her fur stood on end as she pulled out stickers. He crouched down and gloatingly prepared to catch her. BUT! In the twinkling of an eye, she was gone, unaware of her impending doom. Ravenous flailed about, slapping himself up-side the head, grunting and digging up mud with his claws.

"OH! But, WAIT!"

"OH! NO! Purrina's crawling back in his direction! He's reaching for her..."

"Suffern' SNAKES! Come on kitten-cat, jus'-ah-lill' closer, that's it, soooo's-ah-ken'…"

She slipped AWAY.

"SNAKE EYES! FOILED! GONE! Gone! Gone! GONE!
Ah-jus'can't catch NOTHIN'."

He slumped to the ground fantasizing about what he missed.

"Uummmmmm-UMPH! Ta-think ah could-ah-had me some fricasseed KITTEN-CAT, marinatin' in a pot ah snake OIL, frog hips n' raw fish, topped off with a garnish ah weasel juice.

"Humph...ump...ump. Lordy! Lordy-oh-Lordy-dat feline-fur-bag is more slippery-n' angle worms n' ah greasy pan! Dat-could-ah-would-ah-should-ah been good eatin'! But-ah fumbled... Ah jus' had ta FOMBLE!"

He popped himself upside the head as fairy dust circled his nose. He sneezed and gagged, swatting the air.

"AAAAKKKKKK-aaawwa-aaaw-cacacacaca-SKANK-CA- CHU! WATER!!! SKANK WATER! FAIRYDUST! Um-gonna EAT them PESKY vermin!"

He ground his teeth almost to the bones.

"Um gonna 'EAT-UM!! Thems the critters! UM-DA'WOLF! They don't know who they's messin' WITH! I'll grind-um-up in ma- black bean sauce, hog jowls and chitlins, laced with a garish ah shredded cheese an' pickled arugula! CA! CA! CA! CA! Cacacacac...CHU! SKUNK PELLETS!! Them's ain't eatables!! AH can't eat-FAIRIES!"

He began mumbling and crying at the same time.

"Nobody can eat fairies! THEY'S BITTER! An' once yah swallows-um-up...
they pound your innards till ya has-ta-spit-um-out! Ah-choo...ah...ah...Chu!
Um all done-in...um-ah- goner! CA! CA! CA! CA-kitty-cat-cacaca..."

He collapsed in a bed of brambles.

"CHU!"

The fairy dust hit its mark. Slumbering like a baby, he lay in the prickly
bushes, but remember...only for a time. Soon the spell will lose its power and
the wolf will be once again back to his shenanigans.

Chapter Three
The Thicket - Lost and Found

Late that morning, Pancho found Lillabell tangled in the stickers. She was tearfully overjoyed and relieved as he managed to pull and pluck them all away. Upon freeing her wings, they embraced one another.

"Oh Pancho, darlin'! Ah was sooo afraid!"

"Don't worry, my little Chiquita, everything es' going to be alright! Hold on to me...."

After a few moments they began to crawl through the thickest, darkest sticker bushes overhead and underfoot one could imagine. Lillabell could no more fly than Pancho. They wondered if they'd ever find a way out.

"Don't be afraid, hold on to me...don't let go...you are d' roses in d' garden of my eyes!"

It was mid-morning when Peter finally crawled out of the Thicket. He took a deep breath and gazed up at the marshmallow sky. Its rain clouds were all gone. It was a fresh, bright morning. He tried to wipe the dirt and mud from his shoes and overalls, but they would have to dry in the morning sunlight. He could see the familiar trail, just a stone's throw away. Purrina must have found a way out, she must be on her way to Boom Oak by now, he thought.

Just as he was about to head for the path, he heard the signal—it was coming from the Thicket.

"Pow-wow-ug-ah-waga-om-pow-wow! Pow-wow-ug-ah-waga-om-pow-wow."

It was Purrina's little voice. She was still in the Thicket. There was a small opening where he had crawled out. He forced his way back into the twisted brambles, marked the spot with his scarf and crawled toward the sound of her voice until they finally bumped right into each other.

"PETER! Oh, Peter!! I thought I'd never find you."

"JEEPERS! Purrina! Are yah hurt?"

"Just a few scratches."

"Come on, I found ah way out!"

Once back on the path, Peter gave her a sweet kiss and wiped the mud off her whiskers. They dusted each other off as best they could and headed for Boom Oak's Territory. Pancho and Lillabell would surely find them at the old tree. But how was he going to explain all of this to his grandparents, when he wasn't supposed to go near the Thicket and he was only going into the woods for a short visit? They traveled along the dense trail until the sun vanished in all its glory and the moon shone brightly.

"Oh, look! I can see old Boom! We finally made it!"

It was easy to spot the old tree, looming above all the others. Boom was glad to see them. He spread his branches wide and bid them have a good rest. They flopped down and gave Boom's trunk a big hug.

"Oh Boom! Your leaves on the ground feel so good and warm."

"Have no fear, for I will protect you."

"BUT! Have yah seen the Wolf?"

"A night ago, I spied him heading for the Thicket, trying to escape the fairy dust. He'll not be about, rest well in peace." Purrina snuggled close to Peter and brushed some leaves around them for warmth.

"Meew-ow, Oh Peter! Let's stay close together, so's we can gaze up at the stars and fall asleep. I hope Pancho and Lillabell turn up soon."

"They will. You'll see. I wonder what time it is?

"Jeepers! I...I thought I heard Grandpa's flute." Peter yawned and took Purrina's little paw in his hand.

"I...I guess...Grandpa was right."

"Meew-ow, WAIT A MINUTE! don't let's forget this was your idea, don't-cha-know." Purrina twitched her whiskers and snuggled closer to Peter. "Well...it was a lovely day when we started out, if I say so myself, Meew-ow."

"Yah...not a cloud in the sky, an' I made a promise to Grandma an' Grandpa. Now um-never gonna' win my Badge of Honor."

Purrina rubbed her whiskers and licked her paws.

"Well, badge or no badge...I'm proud ah yah. No matter what."

"Really, Purrina, but..."

"Oh, fiddlesticks! Let's just close our eyes and pretend we're home safe and sound, and Pancho and Lillabell can find us." She gave him a big hug.

Fairyfoot's trusted agents, Beatralean and Bendlewood suddenly appear in one of Boom's branches high above. They sing a haunting lullaby as Peter and Purrina fall fast asleep.

The Fairies' Lullaby

I love you an' nothing will harm you.

The stars know I'm close by your side.

Nothing in the darkness to harm us or scare us.

Wait until the sunlight caresses the dew.

I love you the birch trees are whispering

The stars know I'm close by your side.

Nothing in the darkness to harm us or scare us.

Wait until the sunlight caresses the dew.

So close your eyes.

Tomorrow will bring us...

sunlight an' roses,

rain drops and honey dew,

Magical an' miracle sunlight and morning dew...

Only if we just hold on to tomorrow...

Tomorrow tonight...

Showers of fairy dust drift down upon them as Whisper appears.

I love you the birch trees are whispering...

The stars know I'm close by your side.

Nothing in the darkness to harm us or scare us.

Nothing 'til the sunlight caresses the dew...

So close your eyes...

Stars are hovering...

Tomorrow will bring us...

Sunlight an' roses, rain drops and morning dew,

Magical an' miracle fairy dust to comfort you...

only If we just...

Hold onto tomorrow...

Tomorrow tonight...

At sunrise, Peter and Purrina awakened just in time to see Pancho and Lillabell scurrying up the path. They were so excited. Pancho tossed his hat as high as he could and stepped up, to catch it on his head.

"Ay! Ay! AY!!! There you are! It's time for d' celebrations! I was prayin' d' Wolf, he's no gonna fine' YOU!!"

"Mee-ow...we're all safe!! Thank heavens!"

"Oh! Ma-goodness peep! It was simply awful! Ah was in the worst possible situation, wa-ah-said ma prayers over n' over, an' then all of a sudden, there he was, Pancho that is, an now here we are, safe n' sound!"

"Ay! Ay! AY!!! Mother Nature, she is making me loco! Estoy volviendo loco!"

Lillabell giggled and smoothed his feathers.

"Peep he means it's crazy to stay here. Oh ah love it when you talk like that, Pancho darlin' peep! Ah-jus'-get all goose-bumpy all over!"

She pecked his beak with little kisses....

"An' ah-wanna' jus-give you lots n' lots ah-kisses!"

Purrina swished her tail as usual.

"All right enough MUSHY-STUFF! We gotta' get movin'!"

Peter pulled Compus from his pocket. He tapped on its face and it opened its eyes and yawned. It was indignant.

"What is it! Not now, Master! North or maybe South! Oh! West is best! I don't know! Just go somewhere....I'm sleeping."

"Jumpin' Jupiter! Come on Compus! We gotta hurry!"

"MEEE-OW! It's always complaining about nothin'!"

Suddenly there was a rustling in the bushes.

"Saay...what's that in the bushes? Over by that fir tree?

MEEE-OW!! "Why, it's ah...ah...Man-animal."

Peter spun around to see an odd-looking creature coming from behind a tall fir tree. He had the head of a badger and stood upright like a man. He was wearing an odd coat of twigs and leaves, and on the top of his head was a red, pork pie hat. The creature tipped his hat and clicked his heels with a jerk and a twist, bowing profusely.

"Excuse me, young man! I...am Sire Bumbles. Your Compus seems to be out of order. It is my duty to care for lost individuals, and you are lost? Not to worry I have it on good authority. Fairyfoot has sent me to assist you and your little friends."

"Fairyfoot! Where is she? We need her help!"

"In due time, in due time. Now then...I'm to escort you and your little friends to Wickety's dwelling." He took hold of Peter, looking him up and down. Now then, we're off! Step lively, she will give you food and a good night's rest...so that you're fresh to return home in the morning."

Pancho snatched his sombrero off and threw it to the ground.

"QUACK!! Dats-de witch-ang'-I-don-gonna-wanna see de Witch! She has d' worse dispositions ang' nothing to EAT!"

Purrina swished her tail.

"Yah! We've already been there, don't-cha-know!"

"Peep! Peep! Honestly, I simply can't bear the thought of visitin' that Witch again! Na-Pancho darlin'. Jus' don't you be upset."

Lillabell picked the sombrero up and sweetly placed it back on his head. Peter shoved Compus back in his pocket.

"GEE-WILLIKERS, I'm in big trouble when I get home."

Purrina tugged on Peter.

"SAAAAY! It's a shame you didn't get here sooner Mr. ah Mr. BEMBO... Bumbless."

"BUMBLES! Sire Bumbles, if you please."

"Peep! That's exactly what ah was gonna' say. Peep! Ma-goodness, Mr. ah...Sirus BOO, BOO-BUBBLES! It's been ah day an' ah night since we've had anything to eat. Ah-jus' feel soooo faint...OH! MY!"

Bumbles took a very long, stern, look at each one of them as Lillabell dizzily weaved about.

"Nonsense! All the more reason to step lively! Never mind Wickety."

He performed a fancy JIG as he recited an old Mother Goose rhyme— a habit of his.

Cock-a-doodle-do! What is my dame to do? Till Master finds his fiddle-stick, she'll dance without her shoes.

"NOW TIME to make up for lost time! We're off to Fairyfoot's parade. We'll have plenty to eat at the gathering. Go along, all of you! It'll take the rest of the afternoon to reach it but not to worry, an evening parade is always more fun."

Purrina was so excited, leaping and jumping about.

"Yippy! It's not too LATE! FOOD an' ah PARADE!"

"YIPPY!"

He pushed Peter along and shooed the others. It wasn't easy to follow the path. It started and stopped and jigged and jagged. One had to be very careful, for it was strewn with twigs, stickers, and potholes.

However, it was the safest route. The parade was scheduled to end at Fairyfoot's castle in Shadow Creek. After several hours of marching along the trail, Lillabell grew weary once again. She plopped down on a patch of weeds to catch her breath and suddenly noticed a beautiful bouquet of columbines, pink and yellow daisies, and violets, simply out of the blue. Bumbles knelt down for a better look.

"Ah...Fairyfoot. Where e'er she trods, beauty blooms. Those flowers are her footprints, hence the name Fairyfoot."

"HOLY-COW! I guess she's been here an' gone already?"

"I'm afraid so...now come along, Rise-up! She'll be at the parade... you'll see her there."

"Oh, ma-gracious-me-oh my...ah feel faint again, ah do believe ah have a case of the vapors."

Lillabell fainted, of course in Pancho's arms.

"OH! Don't you worry my little chiquitta-cheek-e-boomba! Everything's going to be alright."

He gave her little kisses to revive her. Bumbles was annoyed.

"Nonsense! Pure Nonsense! You seem to have a per-ponderance for DRAMA, MY dear! Step lively!! Don't drag your heels all of you! I'm in charge of those lost and those to be found. We're soon to be at our destination."

A few miles down the path they could see the flags marking the start of the parade. At last they had arrived. A Pixie wearing a golden robe and carrying a trumpet, emerged from behind a clump of trees.

"Alright everyone! It's time for the parade to begin!

Peter, Pancho, Lillabell, and Purrina all arrived just in time to hear him play the trumpet cadence heralding the beginning of the parade. It was so exciting.

Whooping and hollering with delight, they made their way up to the clearing— joining the FAIRIES, ELVES, and BROWNIES along the parade route.

A group of elves and fairies in the trees high above showered a burst of flower petals down on them. The petals danced on the cool evening breeze, and the air was filled with the scent of lavender and roses.

The trees spread their branches to bow as Fairyfoot appeared at the head of the parade on her white unicorn, Tanter. Decorated in silver and gold, he pranced in time to the music, proud and glorious.

The Brownies and Gnomes played their handmade reed instruments, and the Leprechauns proudly marched in their finest green attire.

Fairies and Elves danced their favorite quadrilles. Peter, Purrina, Lillabell, and Pancho were awestruck. It was magnificent.

Onward they marched, through the great Ficklewood Forest, all the way up to Shadow Creek. And there lies the Kingdom of Fairyfoot.

It was midnight when the parade ended. As I mentioned before, the castle lies within the boundaries of Ficklewood Forest. Its turret looms high above the trees. It is a magnificent fortress. At the main entrance is an enormous oak door, five feet wide and twelve feet tall. Fairyfoot is the only one with its secret password. With a flash of magic, the great door opens. It bows in honor of Fairyfoot and her guests as they proceed down the golden walkway, mesmerized by the beauty of the great castle.

Chapter Four
A Feast for the Leprechauns

The ballroom was lavishly decorated. Shamrocks, Irish bells, and heather were all about the large dining area. Golden sassafras and scarlet pimpernel adorned the tables and were beautifully arranged. The guests were greeted with the smells of sweet honeysuckle wine, elderberry cider, Irish potato patties, green peppers stuffed with white rice, olive paté, and hazelnuts.

"But, what about Pee-do...Bumbles an'...an'...da odd-ers?"

They all arrived a bit bedraggled but, they were oh, so very hungry. They were seated at Fairyfoot's table. However, there was one important guest of honor missing.

"WHO?"

Paddy McDougal, King of the Leprechauns. The party couldn't or shouldn't begin without him. Fairyfoot was just about ready to call the party to order when suddenly, into the dining room, like a jackrabbit loose from its cage, comes Paddy. A portly leprechaun wearing a tall, green top hat, green britches with a large hole in the rear and a red waist coat, full of dirt. He trounced about from one end of the table to the other, hollering in a thick Irish accent.

"Bless ME! If I've not seen the DEVIL HIMSELF! I lost me senses FIGHTIN' for-me LIFE! Never in me born days! There-e-was...is eyes flashin' like fire-balls! Comin' round the trunk I was...Boom Oak's, when there he stood...Ah! No! No! Ah, E was crouched...on all fours."

Paddy feverishly swiped his hand across his dirty face and scrambled to a chair next to Fairyfoot. A Leprechaun vigorously pounded his fist on the table.

"Wait a-minute NOW! You're sayin' the WOLF, at the trunk of Boom Oak?"

"Aye, that I am.... Yes."

"At the parade then?"

Paddy scratched his back-end and answered rather meekly.

"Weell...when I was nearin' the parade. E was trackin' me!"

"I saw nothin'. Did you, Finnegan?"

Finnegan continued to stuff his face with potato patties as he spoke.

"If you're askin' did I see the WOLF at the parade, take a bite ah Paddy's britches? When he fell from a tree? Then...prance about with his big teeth an' his wild ways? NO! Imagine ah Wolf will-ya-now, dancin' ah jig at the Parade with the likes of all of us!"

Paddy sprang from his chair, Finnegan shot up from his chair and danced about as if he was the wolf. Everyone howled with laughter. At the height of Finnegan's lampoonist behavior, Paddy yanked his boot off and threw it at him, knocking him upside the head.

"Callin' me a LIAR now are-ya? Ya-PIKER! Twas near the end! At the stroke-ah midnight UM-SAYIN'! I spied-um, lickin' is-chops as if I'm ta-be his next meal! E-took a bite ah me britches! E-did!" Paddy slowly bent over and carefully wiped the mud from his left boot.

"WOOO! TOO BAD ya-didn't wear-yarrr UNDIES!"

He spun around groping his backside, feverously covering it with his hands.

"A pretty Leprechaun!" Bonnie Jean, shouted.

"That's it! There ya-have it! There's the spot!"

Paddy's face turned beet red.

"SAINTS BE BLESSED!"

"Um-afraid the Saints can't help-yah-NOW!"

Finnegan knocked his table settings to the floor, howling with laughter. Fairyfoot tried to call the room to order, but Finnegan sprang from his chair, grabbed a fork and began slapping out a snappy rhythm on the tabletop.

"Ah... ah... now...ear's a little-ditty-far-yah!"

McGROGAN IF YAH PLEASE

Me name's Finnegan Grogan...

McGrogan if ya please,

We're asked to believe,

Paddy rounded a tree,

And Ah Wolf took a bite of his britches...

Now the hole in his britches needs stitches.

Now the hole in his britches needs stitches.

It's not a fine way ta begin your day with a hole in your bum- an' your britches.

Humm T-diddle-Te-dum-HOORAY...

Hum T diddle-T-day!

Hum T diddle-T-day!

A Leprechaun, in the mist of choking with laughter, spit his elderberry cider across the table. Bonnie Jean mopped it up with her hands, shouting:

"NOW! NOW! Mind your manners, O'Leary!"

"We haven't ANY!"

Finnegan tipped his chair and fell over it top-side. Paddy sprang up, not to be out-done.

"AH! SERVES YAH RIGHT FINNEGAN! YA-PIGHEADED LUMMOX!!"

"Mind Your OWN self! Your nose-hairs are longer than me-whiskers."

Bonnie Jean's table settings fell to the floor as she pounded her fist.

"Ha! Ha! Ha! He's RIGHT about that Finnegan! But! Mind yourselves, there's none uglier than that WOLF, if I say so me-self! Except...! PADDY'S FAT BUTTOCKS!!"

Wild laughter spread through the banquet hall. O'Leary, an elderly Leprechaun with a very long beard, leaped onto the table and danced a jig. Bonnie shouted,

"SHAME on the LOT-OF-YAH! EVERYONE Mind your manners!"

"WE HAVEN'T ANY!"

Well...you see Beanie and Farfull, according to Irish folklore, the Leprechauns are a lively bunch of mischievous "sprites" and Fairyfoot had to ring the tiny bell at her place setting for silence.

"Let us not forget this is a celebration in honor of Paddy McDougal, his hard work is well-appreciated. And for all of you, the Leprechauns of County Court, for the planting of the precious Dragonwood Trees, for none can draw as near as all of you, to the frightful Down-Under... except...our own Sire Bumbles."

Finnegan sprang from his chair.

"Let's HEAR it THEN FOR SIRE BUMBLES!"

"HIP! HIP! HOORAY!"

"HIP! HIP! HOORAY!"

Fairyfoot raised her chalice.

"And to you, Paddy McDougal! For we shall never forget your dedication and hard work, for we shall not be caught off guard again. Neither giant nor ogre can escape their watchful eyes."

"May you be blessed with good cheer and a safe crossing home, each and every one of you."

She raised her chalice.

"Here! Here!!"

McDougal sat down calmly, with a smile replacing the sour grimace that crossed his lips a moment ago. With a tap of Fairyfoot's wand, his britches and all of the table settings were good as new.

"Now then, 'tis true, the Wolf is a menace."

Bonnie raised her chalice.

"AYE! That he is! But! Let's be thankful that the giant Morfus is no longer among us."

"Hip-Hip! Hooray!"

Finnegan raised his chalice.

"He's done FOR if I say so me-self!"

Bonnie Jean stood up.

"I'll toast to that!"

Peter shot up from his chair.

"Holy-Toledo! I'll catch that WOLF! I WILL! An' get my Badge of Honor too!"

The room fell silent, Paddy McDougal placed his hand on Peter's shoulder and sat him down.

"Now, now...you're-still-a-wee-bit of a lad. Maybe in a year...or two or three!"

The others chimed in...

"Or TEN! Or twenty!"

Fairyfoot rose from her chair, commanding silence.

"Enough! The Boy has every right to dream. He might make all of us very proud one day."

She smiled at Peter with a great light in her eyes. He felt so much better after receiving such a warm smile.

"Now then, let the music and merriment begin!"

The Leprechauns stuffed themselves with appetizers as elaborate trays of food arrived at their tables. A group of Musicians entered the ballroom and crossed to a special stage in the hall. The leader stepped forward, raising his baton.

"HERE! HERE! Our first medley is dedicated to our gracious host, Queen of Fairies! May she e'er reign! To Fairyfoot!"

"HIP-HIP-HOORAY! HIP-HIP-HOORAY!"

He bowed graciously, stepping forward.

"Tis written in the great book of fairytale anthologies that, where e'er she trods...beauty BLOOMS!"

"Aye! TIS SO! Say I, King of Leprechauns! Tis truth! And rightly so! Rightly so!"

The Musician lifted his fiddle and placing it under his chin, bowed graciously.

"Therefore, here's a tune me-dear-ol' grandma sang to me...ah, No, no... me...me...dear ol' grandfather."

TOURRY-REE-A

As I went walkin' out this day...

Me too-ree-ou-ree-ou-ree-a...

Ah maiden fair with wild green hair

Bid me come her way...

She was a fairy maiden and I did learn her name...

We danced from morn 'til the moon came out...

Me too-ree-ou-ree-ou-ree-a...

Me too-ree-ou-ree-ou-ree-a...

The merriment went on into the wee hours of the morning. When the clock struck 4 AM, Fairyfoot took Peter aside and gave him strict instructions.

"You're to follow Bumbles' advice. Mind what he tells you and do his bidding."

"AH! Gee-willikers!"

"You're not to disobey. There's enough fairy dust about to keep the Wolf confused for a time. Now, you must be on your way."

She gathered them all around. Lillabell, Purrina, Pancho, and Bumbles—and gave them each a package of sweet cakes.

She opened the gate with her magic password and bid them all a safe journey home.

Time marched with a tick and a tock, pulling the sun up, and oh their sleepy faces, how they did long for their warm beds. Sire Bumbles, true to his duty, escorted them safely into the Meadow and then disappeared as usual.

Well...Beanie and Farfull, Peter...as you will learn, was in greater danger when he disobeyed his grandparents and ventured back into the forest. He fell into the dreaded Boog-E-Hole—where the sun don't shine, and the trees don't grow—and was captured by the giants, Morfus and Ortica, enormous gourmet chefs who like to make stew out of children and talking animals. The Hunters—stumbling bumpkins—were useless. They complained fearfully about their loss of hair and appetite encountering the biggest Villain of them all—the ginormous, schizoid, wacked-out, carnivorous eating terror of Ficklewood Forest—Ravenous Wolf.

Stay tuned for the next episode!

Not to worry...this is a tale with spells and prayers, lessons of bravery and the importance of telling the truth.

There now, Beanie and Farfull...I must close the book for today. But, I promise to return tomorrow at the same time, and I hope all of you in storybook land return to hear the next episode.

GLOSSARY

WICKETY

*Bupkes: Plural of goat
   or sheep droppings

*Schmuck: A foolish person

*Mishegas: Crazy

*Schmitzig: Dirty, grimy

*A Klog-iz-mir: Woe is me!

*Oy Vey: Indicating dismay or grief

Cat-got-your-tongue: Speak up

Farafinkel: Author's slang

*Borrowed from Yiddish

PANCHO DUCK

Ay Carumba: Denotes surprise

Ay Chihuahua: Annoyance or
   resignation

Volviendo loco: Driving me crazy

Amigo: A friend

PADDY McDOUGAL

Piker: A person who withdraws
   from a commitment

Pigheaded lummox: Willful, to be
   doing something stupid

Shenanigans: Silly, mischievous

ALLESENDRA

Lampoonist: To ridicule or satirize

Blarney: Overly complimentary
   language

MEET THE ACTORS

Charles Moselle

· Ravenous Wolf
· Foogie Tree
· King Boom Oak,
· various sound effects

Buffy Ford Stewart

· Grandma Piper
· Maple Tree

Rebecca Nile

· Allesendra, the Storyteller
· Purrina Kitten-Cat
· Peter Piper

Esther Clyman

· Nanny Picklesickle
· Otus, a Hunter
· Fir Tree

Margot Elaine Jones

· Beanie Fox
· Lillabell Bird
· Pancho Duck
· North Wind

Jeanne Lauren

· Ortica the Purple Giant

Corinne Kason

· Witch Wickety
· Queen Fairyfoot
· JB, a Hunter

Oscar Salabert

· Grandpa Vernon
· Morphus the Blue Giant
· Farfull Bear
· Bucky, a Hunter

Benjamin Bossi

· Sire Bumbles
· Whisper the Great
· The Larch Tree

Ken Kramarz

· Paddy McDougal
· Murrell, the Hunter

Beneath the Dragonwood Trees: In the Beginning is the first episode of our exciting trilogy!

These wonderful actors comprise the cast of our trilogy. Various characters may appear in some episodes and not in others.

The audiobook of *Episode 1: Beneath the Dragonwood Trees: In the Beginning* includes a bonus interview with author/creator/performer Margot Elaine Jones, and is available through Audible on Amazon.

Episodes 2 and 3 are forthcoming, both as full-length audiobooks and print editions.

ACKNOWLEDGMENTS

"A project like this doesn't drag on for so many years without relying on the kindness, skill, and patience of a whopping amount of stellar human beings."

This is a quote I knocked off from my goddaughter's (Cintra Wilson) insightful book, *Fear and Clothing*. I couldn't think of better words in which to thank everyone involved in this project.

Firstly, in the early years, I must thank Larry Klein, Buffy Ford Stewart, Tatyana de Pavloff, Gini Wilson, and the now deceased and greatly missed, Brian Turner. There is much I could say about these wonderful people but it's another book.

ANGELS

I must thank Jeanne Lauren and her company, Skyana Entertainment, for the early creation of the puppets, Beanie and Farfull, whom I have depicted in the story. I must heap major amounts of thank you's for her continued financial support over the years that has kept this project alive.

Buffy Ford Stewart has been an angel throughout my life. Our parallel, creative journeys come together for the first time in this production. In our teens, we were actors, singers, and dancer hopefuls. Years after meeting one another, we discovered that we had performed in different musical productions under the same director (Les Abbott); had the same vocal coach as Barbara Streisand (Judy Davis); and studied ballet at the famed Stanley Holden Dance Center in Los Angeles. Buffy's mother, Nancy Ford—who was famous for her musical soirées in the lovely hills of Mill Valley, California—introduced us, and we immediately became fast friends.

76

Buffy is a singer, songwriter, poet, and author, as well as the widow of well-known singer/songwriter, John Stewart ("Daydream Believer"). Finally, after much ado...we're performing together.

I was seventeen when I met Corinne Kason, my first theater gal pal. We were performing members in a company called Comedia Repertory Theater in Palo Alto, California. We garnished great reviews in its production of *Once Upon A Mattress*. She was Winifred, and I was the Flying Nightingale of Samarcand. Numerous musicals later, we vowed that we would work together again someday. Corinne went on to become the can-do actress, working in New York Off Broadway, National Tours, and Regional Theatre; in Los Angeles in TV episodes, ADR, soap operas (*Days of Our Lives* for 2 1/2 years), and commercials. We have finally come full circle—uniting for the first time in many years with this production.

I was seven years old, with Joan Crawford bangs plastered to my forehead with gobs of Dixie Peach pomade, when I met my childhood friend Johanne Christmas. Our mothers were great friends and very creative people. Johanne, a writer herself, has been instrumental in helping me map out a course for the completion of my audio and this printed book. I must also thank her daughter, Tracie Christmas, for taking the time to read through the pages and her grandson, Technical Advisor, Avery Christmas, for his help with the QR Readers.

GOOD AS GOLD: My CAST

I am deeply indebted to my wonderful cast—all of whom have super careers in their own rights—who freely gave of their talents. There were weeks and weeks of rehearsals and recording sessions, deep in the rugged hills of Fairfax, California, the heart of "hippy-dom," and that's putting it mildly.

I have been blessed with great company. Lastly, I must thank my lucky stars for the real genius behind the curtain—Charles Moselle—who can brag of working with the likes of Robin Williams in concert and jazz luminaries Stanley Clarke, Stan Getz, Bobby McFerrin, and Eddie Henderson, to name a few. He is truly a one-man band-jack of all trades.

SPECIAL THANKS

To my mother, who first told me that there were "fairies at the bottom of our garden."

My sister Connie Soulé, Jacqueline Shaffer, and Jane Gallagher for their inspiration and encouragement.

A very special thanks to audiobook publisher Becky Parker Geist of ProAudioVoices for believing in this project and for taking me on as a new director/writer/composer. And for the printed book, I wish to thank Book Midwife, Ruth Schwartz for her patience and expertise, along with talented book designer Lorna Johnson.

CREDITS

Written, Directed and Produced: Margot Jones

Music and Lyrics by Margot Jones

Character Design & Illustrations: Margot Jones

Musical Arrangements: Margot Jones / Charles Moselle

Cantata Musical Score: Margot Jones / Charles Moselle

Musician: All instruments performed by Charles Moselle

Engineer: Charles Moselle

Master Mix: Charles Moselle

Associate Producer: Jeanne Lauren

Technical Advisor: Avery Christmas

Margot Elaine Jones Bio Highlights

Director, choreographer, screenwriter, composer, and producer

Her PBS documentary, Encore for Ruby, the story of an American ballerina and the San Francisco Ballet, traveled throughout PBS stations nationwide.

While in Los Angeles, she learned the techniques of screenwriting working at Anlac Productions for renowned Oscar winner, Stirling Silliphant. She studied acting at the Comedia Repertory Theater in Palo Alto and played the student nurse in the now classic film, Harold and Maude.

Charles Moselle Bio Highlights

Musical arranger, recording engineer, musician and character voice actor

Alumnus of the Lee Strasberg Acting Institute and the California Institute of the Arts, multi-talented Charles Moselle has performed in concert with Robin Williams and jazz luminaries Stanley Clarke, Stan Getz, Bobby McFerrin, Eddie Henderson, and Frank Sinatra Jr. to name a few.

OUR MISSION

Margot Jones and Charles Moselle strive to create family entertainment: non-violent, yet thrilling stories, whose main characters grow in some meaningful way, with original worlds that easily lend themselves to sequels.

They are comedy and/or action stories that will make kids laugh and dream, as well as offer universal themes about friendship and personal responsibility that all families can support.

Episode 1:
Beneath the Dragonwood Trees: In the Beginning
is the first episode of our exciting series!

Look for these upcoming further adventures!

Episode 2:
Beneath the Dragonwood Trees: Into the Boog-E-Hole

Episode 3:
Beneath the Dragonwood Trees: The Journey's End